I0611455

R. Barrett and Sons

A Handbook for Greek and Roman lace making

R. Barrett and Sons

A Handbook for Greek and Roman lace making

ISBN/EAN: 9783742803665

Manufactured in Europe, USA, Canada, Australia, Japa

Cover: Foto ©Andreas Hilbeck / pixelio.de

Manufactured and distributed by brebook publishing software
(www.brebook.com)

R. Barrett and Sons

A Handbook for Greek and Roman lace making

A HANDBOOK

FOR

GREEK AND ROMAN

LACE MAKING.

LONDON:
Printed by
R. BARRETT & SONS, 13, MARK LANE,
1869.

A HANDBOOK

FOR

GREEK AND ROMAN LACE MAKING.

——⋙⋘——

THE art of Lace Making, or rather " Point Lace " Making
(so called, though not very correctly), has of late years been
growing into a favourite one among ladies, and many a beautiful and elaborate imitation of quaint old lace has been the
result. But a less fortunate result is that many magazines,
only too glad to recognise and stimulate any new fashion, and
always ready to supply an endless number of patterns for the
newest styles of work, have undertaken to produce and send
to all their subscribers an overwhelming number of most
plausible-looking designs well filled up with drawn stitches.
And these patterns, having for the most part a familiar and
easy flow of lines—often of flowers and leaves—at once attract
a neat worker, who is thus induced to spend her time and
work upon patterns which are sadly at fault after all, and
really not worthy of the care and patient perseverance so often
bestowed upon them. At the same time it is only fair to
add that, under some clever and ingenious fingers, even these
otherwise faulty patterns become the foundation for such
exquisite work that they assume a character of their own,
and are very beautiful: the only pity being that a more
worthy design was not at first chosen, upon which to devote
so much ingenuity and neatness, so that the result might
have been perfect in its origination as well as in its execution.

There is one great mistake in many, I might almost say in most, of the patterns which are sold, and looked upon as copied from old designs or laces, which patterns however any one with an eye for such things would, on a very slight examination, at once recognise and pronounce as merely a very modern *braid pattern*, and as such very unsuitable for a reproduction of those fanciful and grotesque **designs** which are met with in old laces.

We are in the present day so **accustomed to take the** assistance afforded us, even in our needlework, by machinery —that wonderful *multum in parvo*—that it has become almost unnatural and impossible to refuse the aid, thrust upon us, as it were; and we become unwilling to do as our great-grandmothers before us did, that is, to spend *time* rather than money upon our work. Many, therefore, who really enjoy working, and have taste and time enough to produce pretty and even elaborate works, are sadly apt to be satisfied with patterns brought before them without any trouble by their monthly magazines, though these patterns are evidently planned merely to sell well, and more on the principle of " quantity not quality " than with any attempt at originality, or even a praiseworthy copying from the old designs. We have no right here to quarrel with the more prominent design, nor its result, which leads to an increasing demand for braid, thread, and expensively-drawn patterns on coloured kid, on which the very poorest of patterns just " started " by a work-woman, and often very carelessly started, looks certainly most tempting to a young beginner in the art of lace-making; but there is a higher knowledge and skill gained by experience, which soon detects the weakness of the style, and brings some criticism to bear upon the designs, and then it is astonishing how few really good patterns there appear to be in the great number met with.

The quantity of narrow braid, so easily produced by machinery, has led to a habit of suiting the pattern to the braid, instead of following the old, and certainly more laborious method of suiting the braid or work to the pattern decided upon beforehand. Yet surely such a habit must greatly diminish the originality of the designs, for by using a continuous braid one becomes so tempted to braid a quantity at once without cutting the braid, that soon such patterns as would require it to be cut often are looked upon as too troublesome; although even with such an even braid very pretty designs can be worked with good effect, if done in separate pieces joined together by means of needlework.

But much of the old lace, which our modern "point lace" aims at imitating, was formed with a curious braid, differing much in width every here and there, and having also all manner of holes, or rather strange "faults" and irregularities, utterly impossible to be imitated by machinery, yet giving the decided character of self-prompting to the lace; and this peculiarity is quite unattainable where the foundation of any design is formed of a perfectly regular and even braid though made on a pillow.

It is evident that many of the old braid lace designs were first most carefully traced on parchment, and then the braid was woven upon a cushion to follow and suit the pattern, the width at any place being regulated according to the fancy of the worker, whose individual taste was thus brought to bear on every part of her work, from the very commencement of it. And, consequently, there were none or few of those unsightly and clumsy gatherings at the corners of the design

now observable, and a uniform thickness of texture was
preserved throughout. Where these gathered corners did
however occur, they were not in the finest and most carefully
made laces. There were also patterns of which the foundation certainly was a continuous even braid, and which appears
to have been laid on and worked together, and filled up much
in the same manner as our own modern braid work is done.
But these laces are by no means the most beautiful, or the
most fine or valuable, in so far as neither so much time, care,
nor ingenuity was needed to produce them.

These remarks do not of course apply to any but the
simple flat braid-lace, for a variety in the thickness, as well
as in the width of the foundation, was sometimes added, and
even heavy rolls of work, solidly laid over whalebone, were
often used in order to add richness of effect and weight.
This is the case with " Venetian Point " lace, which is most
wonderfully and thickly adorned in this manner.

Braid made on a pillow is, indeed, now very generally used
for lace-work, but it is made in such a flimsy loose way that
it is almost invariably destroyed by the mere fact of the
stitches depending upon it drawing the threads aside, and
unless great care is taken it soon looks dragged and ugly.
When, however, the braid is very carefully and rather
heavily made, and with casual holes and irregularities, which
pillow-workers will sometimes undertake to make as they
work, it becomes an invaluable aid to the making of braid-
lace; and it must be remembered that where a certain
amount of personal attention and interest can be devoted to
the making of the braid, a far greater success will be insured
afterwards in the production of the lace than if the common
pillow-braid of a flimsy texture be used. Above all, machine-

made braid must be avoided in this style of lace, because, having a plaited appearance, it is altogether unsuitable. Pillow-made braid, though almost rivalling machinery in regularity, is much to be preferred, and some pains should be bestowed upon the choice of a pattern. For work which, if properly done, will last for many years, and which may perhaps be handed down for many generations by loving hands, is surely worth bestowing some trouble upon at first.

In guiding the judgment in the choice of a design, the one point I wish most to impress is, that any mere braiding pattern should not be tolerated as a foundation for a good imitation of old lace, though in itself it may have a very pretty effect.

Enough has now been said on the subject of this particular style of lace, as I do not intend to go into details and descriptions of the many beautiful and intricate stitches which have been already so well described and taught by Mdlle. Riego, in her last book of stitches. This book I should recommend to all those who are fond of this braid lace-work. There are, however, many other kinds of lace which are quite as beautiful and easy of imitation, or rather of *manufacture*, as the so-called " Point Lace," requiring only more patience and care, because the process is certainly slower, and the quantity produced much smaller in the end. But by the simple fact of more time and attention—and if possible of originating thought—having been bestowed upon any work, that work in my opinion becomes more valuable, and more worthy to be called a work of art, in days when people have become so economical of time that few think of making any great outlay of so valuable a thing upon mere fancy work ; and the greater number therefore prefer to employ their

spare moments on some work which will grow rapidly under
their fingers, and in a short time produce the greatest quantity of result.

Now, *quantity* certainly has its own value, which every kind
maker of endless edgings and trimmings for children's frocks
and pinafores can fully appreciate ; but the accumulated gift
of spare half-hours (not necessarily to the exclusion of more
rapid work) upon some really beautiful piece of work, will
amply reward the care and patience spent upon it.

Some years ago a piece of very pretty Corfu lace, curiously
worked in lozenges upon coarse linen, was lent to me, and I
admired it so much that I was seized with a desire to find out
the process by which it was made. My first attempts at
imitation, I need hardly say, were hideous ; but, having my
attention fairly drawn to it, I greedily accepted the loan of
every piece of Greek or Roman lace offered to me ; and at
last I made such progress in the art, that my former favourite
braid, lace, or "lacet" work, seemed to lose all its charms,
and since then Greek lace alone has been my pride ; for I
believe that, as yet, there are a few little secrets of the art
which, having learnt only from the real lace itself, I have
mastered perhaps better than others, at least as far as practice
goes. Among them, for instance, are those cunning little
knots which add such richness to the bars in the braid-lace.
These occur so frequently in the Greek laces, that I could not
rest satisfied with the "recipe" for them given by Mdlle.
Riego ; as also the laces before me had always little stiff
straight knobs, of such an extremely neat form that the old
way of making them would not do at all. Many a trial I
made, and many a little piece of some patient nun's work did
I ruthlessly unpick, in order to discover her secret, before I

succeeded; and now these little knots are the beauty of my work, and after all not difficult to make. The secret, however, must wait until the proper time and place has come, before it is divulged; and we will now take up a piece of lace and begin at the beginning.

At the first sight, Greek or Roman lace appears to be made without any foundation, and almost as if all the parts were done *at once*, and therefore only to be imitated with the greatest difficulty. But a little patience and examination will soon be amply rewarded, and the tiny little squares of woven linen, consisting sometimes of only four or five threads of warp and woof, which will be discovered after a little search, disclose the secret of the groundwork at once.

The first process of making this Greek or Roman lace was a most tedious and monotonous task, and consisted in drawing out certain threads from the coarse linen which was to form the foundation for the needlework afterwards.

Let us now try to make a small square of lace, such as will be seen drawn on the next page. This was drawn from a piece sold by Helbronner some years ago, and which struck me as so like a piece drawn in Mrs. Bury Palliser's delightful " History of Lace," that it deserves a place of honour here, and will serve us now as a very good example of the lace we are speaking of. We would begin by taking a piece of the coarse linen, somewhat larger than the square to be worked. The border is made by drawing out three or four threads in such a manner as to mark out the square, and then finishing the edge by rolling it up firmly, and then hem-stitching it neatly and regularly down with rather coarse linen thread, beginning at the left-hand corner and working on the wrong side, or that on which the rolling will be seen.

This figure will now represent the appearance of the
border. The next thing to
be done is to draw out three
or four threads a little below
and in the same direction,
and hem-stitching over the
little strip of linen thus left
in the centre of the two sets

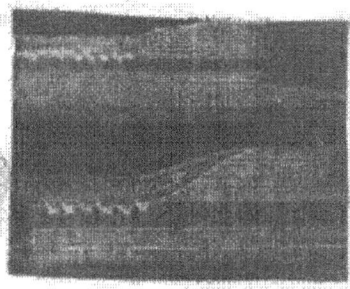

of perpendicular threads. This will be more easily under-
stood if a piece of linen, a needle and thread, be taken in

hand at once, when, by being
careful to begin at the left hand
and working towards the right,
the result is sure to be successful. *See* Fig. 2.

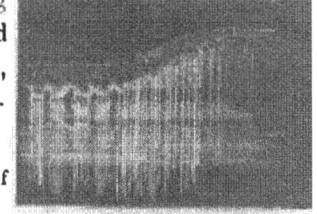

N.B.—This shows the wrong side of
the work.

Figs. 3 and 4 will explain at once the next steps to be
taken, and the manner in which to proceed. Great care
must be taken to use very sharp scissors, and on no account
to cut more than is intended, as cutting even one thread of
the foundation, to be left after the other threads are with-
drawn, will often prove a serious trouble when the " Cluny "
stitch has to be done.

The principal foundations being now fairly established, we
will find that in many designs diagonal supports are also
needed. These diagonal lines may be thrown across with
the needle ; two or three threads (according to the place
where you wish to end) will generally be found sufficient to
begin with. After these threads have been thrown across,

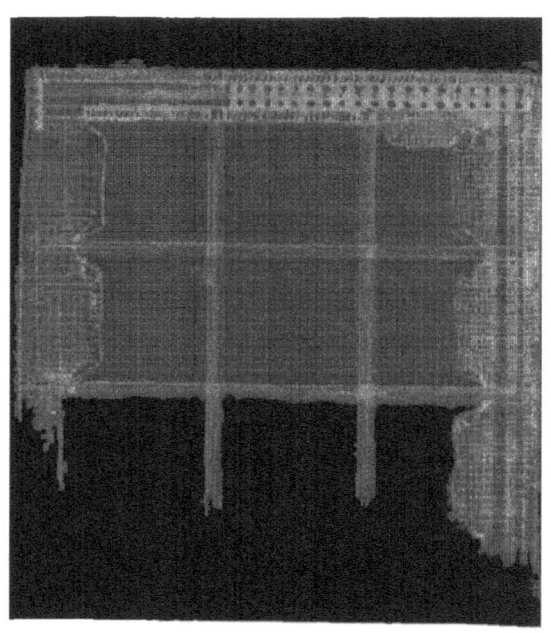

they must be covered by carefully working over and over them, taking pains that only the thread in the needle bends and rolls round, and not the foundation threads. If the foundation threads twist at all, the result is like a rope, in which all the strands are equally twisted; but if the inner threads are kept firm, the whole when finished carefully should present this appearance :—

The work is now fairly started, and ready for the further additions of patterns, which often are very symmetrical if carefully examined, although at first sight they appear very irregular and complicated.

This irregularity, which is one of the chief beauties of the Roman or Greek laces, arises more from the different *tension* given to the foundation threads, by which means they are pulled to one side or another by the work, afterwards depending upon them, far more than from any great variety of pattern. A very stiff-looking pattern on the working paper need not, of necessity, when worked produce a stiff and formal piece of lace. Thus a clever and ingenious worker, by no very great pains, may easily succeed in producing a prettily curious and varied effect from a simple and almost formal and geometrical pattern.

We now come to the stitches which were used to form the more solid parts of the work. And here a very few lessons will teach all that is necessary, for in this kind of lace there was not that endless variety of stitches which make the beauty of all point laces. And the one chief way of filling up any shape desired in this lace was to add line upon line of that stitch which is commonly known as button-hole stitch, and, in French embroidery terms, "feston"; the "point d'echelle," or ladder stitch, was also often used, and a stitch which, being frequently found in Cluny laces, we will call the "Cluny stitch," sometimes done on two, sometimes on three, foundation threads :—

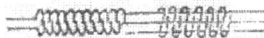

And then the little knots which form a sort of fringe to the solid parts and are sometimes very thickly placed together.

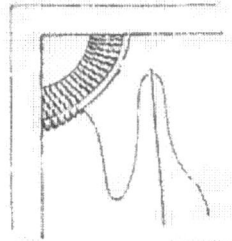

Suppose that we wished to make a solid band of work in a corner, thus— We would begin by throwing across from *left to right and back again* a foundation thread, which for the first row should always be double. Now feston a row of stitches until you have covered your foundation; but be careful not to place the stitches too close together. Then throw back another single thread, so as to make the foundation for the next row, and also to enable you to begin again at the left hand. Now work one stitch into each one of the first row, and cover the new foundation thread till you again reach the right-hand end of your band. This process you must repeat until you have formed a band of work sufficiently wide for your purpose, and then you will probably wish to end it off with a few knobs. But it does not always happen that you have such a convenient border or corner in which to fix your work, and often an odd-shaped piece must be done "en l'air," so to speak. By the same process of always throwing back a new foundation thread for each row, and by carefully considering where to place this thread in the last row, and where to end each row, you will soon be able to make a piece of almost any shape. If the piece to be made is *very* large or very curiously shaped, I would, as I worked, fasten it down to my pattern with some fine silk to keep it well in its place till the real supporting bars can be fastened. But you will not find this often necessary, unless you are copying a piece of old lace with really no easily defined foundation lines to which to attach your work. In such a case it is well to draw your pattern with all its irregularities as nearly as you can, and then to stitch down such *bent* foundation lines as you can find before beginning. And then proceed piecemeal to support the work as you go on. This is very laborious, and a great deal of beautiful lace may be done without it.

We will now learn how to make the little knobs. When firmly and neatly executed, these little additions are wonderfully successful, far more so than the loose round knots or knobs which are generally taught by the samples in the "begun pieces of point lace." We must go back to our last row of the little band of solid feston work, and having as usual thrown back the foundation thread, three or four stitches must be made as before, beginning of course from the left. Then make one more stitch, but instead of drawing it up close, place the left hand thumb on the left hand thread of the loop, and hold it very firmly down upon the pattern, while with

the right hand make the *needle* twist the thread of the other side of the loop six times round itself (*i.e.* the needle). Now place the needle under the left-hand thumb and draw up the thread A until the coil and needle are both brought close up to the last row of the feston, and then the whole of your work so far will be concealed and firmly held under your thumb and the first finger on the other side. Be very careful that your thread was not too tightly twisted round the needle, or you will find some difficulty in the next step. Take hold of the point of the needle, and draw it with the thread attached right through your six loops, being very careful not to move your left thumb during the process. There may be a

few troublesome knotty pieces of thread (if your thread is long) which will almost baffle your attempts to draw them through your coils. But you must steadily and patiently unroll or unknot them, and pull the whole length of the thread through without disturbing the little coils under the thumb, which you may now raise, and the result should then present the appearance of this little figure.

If, on the contrary, one little knot gets down between your finger and thumb the knob is lost, and must be started again. You will see that now the thread A has taken the place of the needle, and as soon as you take it with your right hand you will see that the thread B (the other side of your original loop) will at once begin to make a reverse coil round the first one, and this is just what we want.

Now begin very slowly to pull up the thread with your
right hand, and encourage the outer
coil of B by rubbing it with your left
thumb in the direction of that coil,
pushing your thumb from left to right
while the coil lies upon it, until by
means of these two contrary twists,
and the gradual shortening of the
thread A, a regular little pillar of
rope ending in a single thread, which
comes out of its centre, is produced,
like that seen on the right of the
last little figure. Now make one
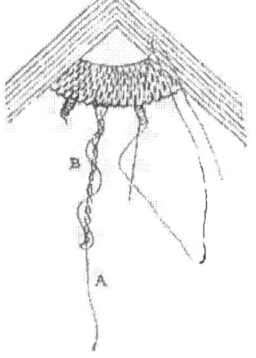
more feston stitch in the same stitch as the last, and leave
your little pillar standing straight out, having at the back
only one straight thread leading from the top of the pillar
to the work. This single thread should be carefully pushed
to the back so as not to be seen at all on the right side of
the work, and the little knob is finished. If this process
is not really attended to, you will find that you have two
untwisted threads behind, and the knob will not be firmly
coiled, nor keep its position well.

When you have succeeded in making these knobs well,
and the piece of solid feston work very evenly, and the cluny
stitch, and the even-coiled rope for diagonal foundations
(these two may sometimes for a variety be done in the cluny
stitch), and the two equally-twisted threads (*point d'echelle*)
for lighter bars, you have learnt sufficient to do any pattern;
needing only the aid of a little ingenuity and practice to show
you *which* foundation lines to throw across first, and which to
tack down firmly to your pattern to prevent their being drawn
out of their places *too soon*.

They must be allowed to be drawn aside a little (having on purpose not set them too tightly at first) that the work may not look too geometrical, but this is so unavoidable that you will need great care that this does not happen too soon, or you will not find place for your stitches.

You will now find that the very tedious and laborious task of making all your foundations conscientiously on drawn linen, takes really far more time than any young lady, who has other things to do, can fairly devote to such mere preliminaries; for it is to be remembered that the nuns and others who worked the originals, had far more leisure than ladies have now-a-days.

As every one likes to be able to produce a certain quantity of pretty work in a reasonable time, I think we may shorten the *foundation* work considerably without much injury to the after effect; though, where there is perseverance and time, the accomplishment of one little square done in the old way will be the source of real pleasure, and never to be regretted. Having, however, learnt on this little square, we will condescend to a FEW short cuts; but the less the better. For instance, we may greatly shorten the *foundation* work without much injury to the general effect. And this I would do by procuring a very narrow linen braid, if possible of a rather coarse, *darned* kind, which has been made by hand; in fact a sort of linen *tape* would be best. This should be tacked down on either side of your insertion-pattern, or if not an insertion it should be tacked along the longest single line to be found, using some discretion in the choice of the line. And this tape should be only used in sufficient quantity *just* to afford a firm line from which to throw across as many foundation threads covered with cluny-stitch or the rope-stitch as are necessary for the work in hand. In general the *cluny*-stitch should be used for such foundation lines as would represent linen, the *coil* ones being used in preference for diagonal foundations. This is not, however, to be looked upon as a RULE by any means, as the cluny-stitch may be used in any direction; the only point always to be borne in mind being that you are supposed to be working on linen. Where cluny foundation-lines cross at right angles, and in the direction of your supposed linen, it would have a very good effect if you did a few darning lines so as to represent the threads of woof and warp left at those little squares in the old process of drawing the linen away.

But it is worth while, where a good piece of lace is begun which is not to be too fine, to make at least a true linen edge, such as may be seen in one of the Roman laces, drawn with the linen border hanging from it, and then to use the needle and thread foundations only for the inner work to depend upon.

There now only remains to be described the way of finishing off the edges for either insertions or larger pieces of work. In Mrs. Bury Palliser's "History of Lace" there are given a few exquisite specimens of what are called *petites dentelles*, which would give a charming finish to an insertion. But even simpler border laces would have a very pretty effect, and are by no means difficult of execution; and provided they are rather *tightly* and firmly done, they will preserve their form and position very well, and are well worth adding.

The drawings which will be found in this little hand-book, are all quite simple, and may be easily worked; and many pretty insertions, on borders or squares, to be alternated with little squares or oblongs of new-stitched linen, may be arranged from them. There is also a *skeleton* pattern drawn, in order to show how to set about marking out a piece of lace preparatory for working, as of course it would be quite as useless as tedious to draw it out more elaborately.

There is a kind of transparent calico which, I believe, is called *tracing cloth*, used for drawing plans, &c., upon, and to be procured at the stationers; and on this cloth the patterns may be neatly and clearly drawn in ink, and then tacked down to any rather stiffer stuff, and bound round with a little ribbon. This kind of lace requires rather a stiffer support in the working than the soft kid on which braid patterns are usually drawn; and it will not be found a very troublesome undertaking to draw a short piece of the skeleton pattern on the tracing cloth, mounting it firmly afterwards.

Having now given a description of the manner in which to work Greek or Roman lace, I hope these few instructions may prove clear enough, with the help of a needle and thread and a piece of linen, to explain all such little difficulties as there may be in the art, and that the specimens I have drawn may induce many to attempt their imitation.

R. BARRETT & SONS, Printers, Mark Lane, London.

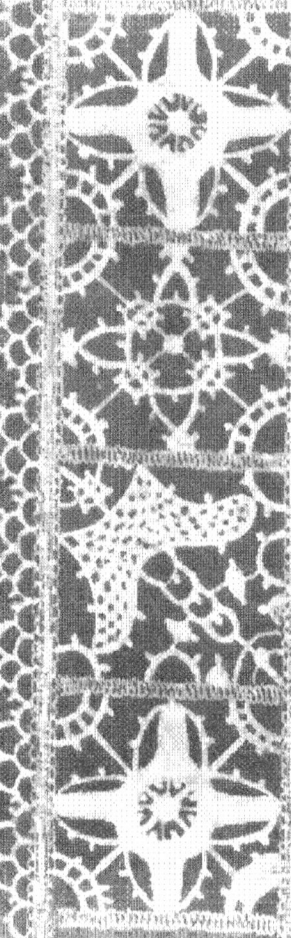

cuttings from ... ...

1594   date 1598   1598

Papier dentelle

From Roman

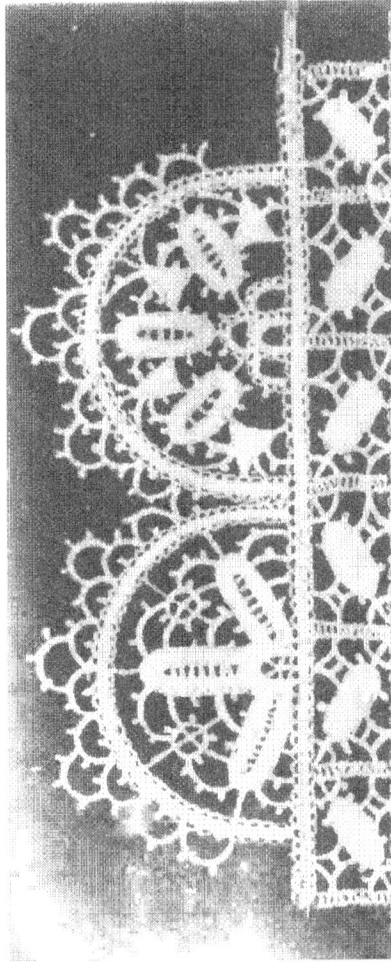

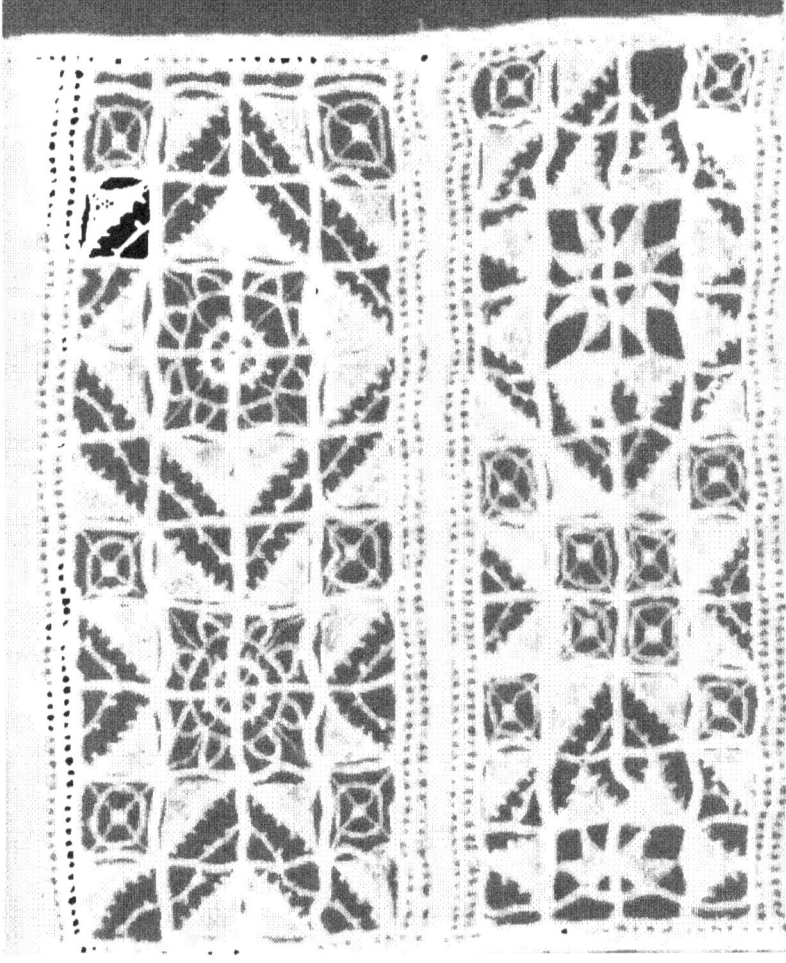

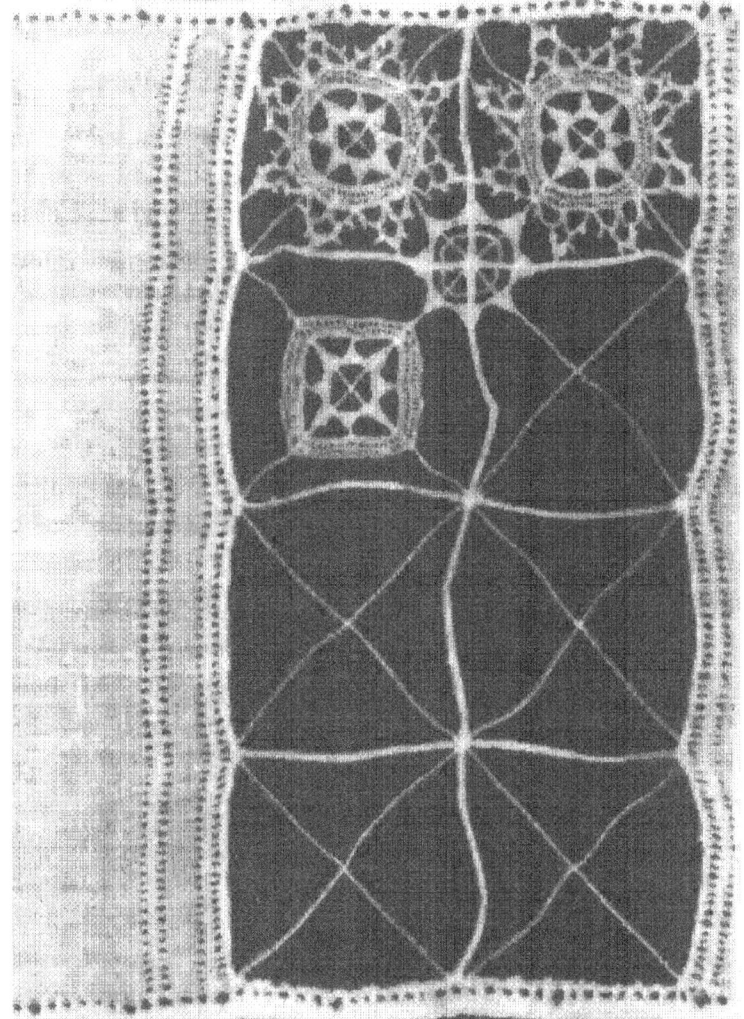

www.ingramcontent.com/pod-product-compliance
Lightning Source LLC
Chambersburg PA
CBHW031334070726
47496CB00018B/2814